Seeking Sex Without Armor

Nik Nicholson

BaileyGirls Publishing LLC
www.baileygirls.com

First Selection and Editor: Claudia Moss
Second Selection and Editor: Nik Nicholson
Grammar and Line Editor: Katy Skipper
Copy Editor: Nik Nicholson
Cover Painting: Nik Nicholson

Published by Bailey Girls Publishing LLC
12/15/2015

www.baileygirls.com

ISBN: 978-1-942037-04-0

For each of us
Courageous
Or foolish enough
To seek love
To embrace love
To leave love
To learn love
To teach love
To speak love
To be love.

Seeking Sex Without Armor

Introduction

From What I Remember

Closet Poems

Dating

Prospects

Breaking Up

Rebound Poems

Relating

Introduction

Peace,

Selecting poems for *Seeking Sex Without Armor* was a mesmerizing, painful, and spiritual journey. These poems were selected from many written between 1998 and 2015. So many decisions. How vulnerable should I be? Why is one love poem more important than another? How many poems should I include? If I don't feel this way about dating and love now, should I include these poems from my past? Do I know enough about love, connection and sex to share my experiences? Should I write more poems to balance this collection out?

After sitting with these questions, I realized I wanted to control how I was perceived. I also acknowledged I am afraid of judgment.

My favorite writers never claimed to know everything. Their transparency allowed me to hurt, heal and grow with them. They made the intangible possible. As a writer, I hope others will evolve with me.

Love is life. Live.

From What I
Remember

in poem pieces giving myself away

i don't remember
the intonation or timbre
of the first word i understood
or articulated
or the first time i found a sound
i could identify with
or the first time a poet, a poem, a sequence of words
made my heart stop like love does
and for a moment
it was euphoria
pinched in the wind
and time was tactile
enough to inhale.
but i do remember the first time
i was beaten for cursing
or the way the wrong word
from my mouth
as a child
brought the whole room to a halt.
i have said tons of things, i regret.
i can never take back secrets
i wish i'd kept.
i wish i had more silence than regret
more silence than guilt.
i wish i had more of myself…
but then again
i was always a poet
and poets must surrender
their silence
to relate
to everyone else.

School taught us
We are reproductive systems
Like the solar system
Made our bodies intergalactic.
Jupiter, the largest planet
With the strongest gravity
And 63 known moons.
No mention of love, feelings
Or emotional pull.
No mention of orientation
Or gender presentation
Nothing spiritual.
Made us mechanical and common.
Made us Neanderthals.
Him man, me woman.
Male: penis, erection, orgasm, ejaculation, semen,
sperm
Swimming for eggs.
No mention of man between woman's legs.
No mention of the interpersonal
Consent
Or her opening
To welcome him.

Venus
Second planet from the sun
Searching for her one.
Seen with the naked eye for centuries.
Once named Lucifer, meaning
Bringer of light.
The brightest and hottest planet in the sky.
Rotating
In her own direction

Ovulating.
No mention
Of female ejaculation
Just penetration.
School taught us
Female objectification
Vagina, ovaries, fallopian tubes
Uterus, womb
Baby
Cervix dilating
Procreation.

Trigger warning

an uncle
was the first
to teach me about sex
whenever i was left
for him to babysit.

i am 3 or 4
in the earliest memories
haunting me.
it happened
many times before
i could physically remember.
when i can remember
i am already familiar
with the routine.
hurt, i know not to scream.
still he threatens me
before and after
maturing me.

when i was 14
he apologized.
around 28 or 29
he tells me
he isn't a pedophile
defining himself as "also a child."
just a male teen
with a girl doll
hormones demanded he inspect
anatomically correct
anatomically correct
again and again
he had to check

he had to check
with his fingers
with his dick.

Songstress
Betray our sisters
Who sing only of lost love
Or their journey to find love.
So young girls will no longer dance
To longing
Possessed by spirits
Loving others
Hating themselves.
Ignite our fire
To fulfill our own desires
And journey to find our own selves.
And love our reflections
The way God intended.
Let us know
Each perceived flaw
Is the infinite's perfection.
Sing lessons
Hard learned
Bruises earned
That they may never be my own
But please
Don't sing us another sad love song.

love taught me
it's difficult to speak
especially when asked,
"what do you mean?"
trying not to be mean
misconceived
or words
or sound
though discontent is loud.
trying
to hear what is to be heard
not dazed by every single word
sifting for content
grasping at facades
we put on and take off.
struggling to keep on
and not get lost.
bruising and beating
egos
breaking
masks
without holes for breathing
revealing
souls'
beaming
light
freeing.
sometimes definitions are wounded
in the healing.

i try to stand up
without stepping on anyone's toes
haven't always managed
balance
haven't mastered balance.
sometimes i fall.
sometimes i
waver
sometimes i am dizzy.
just when my hands are slipping
or something's too heavy to hold
i impress myself
and never let go.
or respect it's
time to let go.
beyond forgiveness or blame
on to something more concrete
like
behavior change.
still dealing with
guilt and shame
so i comfort myself saying
falling
is just an aspect of life
to alert us to imbalance.
sometimes i stand immediately
sometimes i rest
think about some shit
how i got here.
then i stand
again
the dance
balance

knowing
i will fall again.

against the grain
i was 18
a fearless fool with an over-inflated ego
easily deflated
how many ways did i hate me
before i knew
what the apprehension really was
or better yet, what it wasn't
some fact that women don't like sex
made it about the sex
not the actors
made me not a human
but a character
acting out who i was taught to be
acting out what was expected of me
acting out 'cause i hated to be
touched
acting out 'cause i hated the idea of us
acting out 'cause i didn't like the prospects of love
before knowing
my spirit was screaming, "NO!"
just to men
and not love.

Couldn't Say I, Never Knew

I always loved the truth told by liars
Taught to hate passion and desire.
God was
Is
My eternal father.
Me always needing a good chastising
Suicidal
Taught to ignore this life and
Live for dying
Store up my treasures in the sky and
I was
Just a
Silver-tongued man's fool.

Could have been a prostitute
But I was much too astute
To live my life
Literally being defiled.
So I joined the other 95% of you whores
Except I won't be bending over in denial.
Which makes the degree of the burns
Even deeper
Every time
Every time
Every time I
Choose the fire.
Cause I
Couldn't say I
Couldn't say I
Never knew.
I knew what I was

Walking into.

I could never follow rules
Paths
Or roads
Never could put my heart into reaching
Superficial goals
I was always cutting across the grass
Guiltily running from my past
Looking for a detour
Shaking knobs on doors
Hoping it would open an orb
To absorb this
Urge
To keep searching for
More.
And give me that familiar feeling
Like
I've been here before.
But it seems like
You lose so much time
When you don't just
Stay inside the lines.
Seems like
You lose so much light
When you don't just
Follow what's inside.
That path
Is divine.

So I don't cry when I'm lost.
Or curse life
When it's time to pay the cost.

'Cause I've learned
To appreciate my scars
As badges of honor
And testaments to the wars
Lost and won
For survival.
I don't beat myself up
When I'm tired, too exhausted from fighting
And can't be ignited
No matter how you light it.
Though something is not right and
Not fair
I can't care
Or be confused.
Thankful
When my knees are just scraped
And I've escaped
With no broken bones and
Just a little bruised.
'Cause it's not manipulation when
You know you're being used.
And I
Couldn't say I
Couldn't say I
Never knew
I knew what I was
Walking into.

Closet Poems

Crushing Before Coming Out

Heartbeat
Drumming
In my throat
Anchoring my tongue.
Sound deserted
Your name
Left it
Barely audible
Conjuring
An abyss between us.
Condemned to hell
If I admit
I'm attracted to you, woman.
Woman,
I am baptized.
Saved.
Sanctified.
I am bound
Passion
Suffering
To do more
Than acknowledgments
Say more than pleasantries
Give more than greetings in passing.
Tired
Of passing,
For straight.

<u>Out?</u>

"I just can't do that to my family
I could never come out"
She is pleading more than explaining
"I love them and they would never understand"
She repeats to herself
Internalizing rejection
I'm meditating
On the conversation pushing us apart.

Instantly, we are friends
If even that.
Letting go I brace myself
For what she is going to ask.

After the silence has blessed our separation
She rises to the occasion, with this sad tone
Directly she wants to know
"Would you ever date someone who isn't out?"

The way she asks
Paints her victim of circumstance
Me villain
And answering "no"
Abandonment.

I'd feel guilty
Had I never been asked before.

All I have are questions for her question.
How would you introduce me to your mother
If you can't call me your partner, woman, girlfriend

or lover
What will you call me?
And do you expect me to answer?

If another out woman comes along
Who affirms her love
Will you be threatened and desperate?
Possessive and jealous?
Do you want me to tell her who you are
What we are?
Would you want to be acknowledged, my love?
Will you then find it in yourself to claim me
To properly name me
And then
Do you expect me to also answer?

Would you ever pretend you never knew me at all
Depending on who's around and what I've got on?
Will you whisper when I call?
How can we live together
Or have a family together?
Do you expect me to stage our dwelling
Pretend this is your room, and that one is mine
Every time people come by?
And if they spend the night
Do you expect us to sleep apart?
Do you expect me to stand idly by
While your family plans your life?
What of children?
Will you ever bare mine
Or let me have yours?
And how will you claim them?

What will we name them?
How will they know to answer?

Will you hold my hand in public?
Who will you tell you love me?
Should it be enough that I know?
Should I lie for you?
Should I hide with you?
Should I tell my family you are mine
But to deny you, too?
So they never acknowledge you
When it is inconvenient.

I understand
You could never hurt your family.
So are you asking me to agree
To let you hurt me?

Dating

first date

bracing
to step forward
barefoot
on broken glass
with soles in various stages of healing.

i don't tell her everything.

i've learned
it is socially unacceptable
to serve a heavy meal
before appetizers.
i don't tell her how much i want her
because it's a turn off to eat like you're starving
even when hungry.

i don't tell her everything
because people are matches
struck
and wicks
needing to be lit
to see how they burn.

i don't tell her everything
because i've read somewhere
and been told thousands of times
i should never tell any one person everything
nor should i be too open with my secrets.
in fact, girls should always keep a few things to
themselves.

even years later
after i've learned-
"secrets" is a metaphor for "virginity"
guilt ridden i gave me away literally
too young and underpriced.
i'm haunted by intangible warnings
i needed to grasp
while i was reaching faithfully

outside of myself
and letting him in.
i don't tell her everything
trying to repay the past
relay the path
and stop following "him."

"God"
defined by man.
men, treated like gods
and me waiting
for salvation.
i thought he was a savior
the way he smiled
and curled his lips
grown women
taught me to worship men.
encouraged me to worship him
and put everything before myself
while ignoring how scripture
contradicted itself
and gave fathers instructions for selling daughters
as slaves.
sex slaves?
sex slaves.
i was told i lacked faith
for questioning.
i was seeking a leader
to head my household
i was seeking an escape
from my hole.
i was seeking a piece
to make me whole

but all i did was fall
deeper
into the silence of my soul
and break into more pieces.
the teaser, pleaser
an obedient sanctified breeder
a subject seeking to be an object
in the context
of her drama.
i don't tell her everything.

i don't tell her everything
because lovers' utterances
become colorful inlets
on the canyons of our spirits.
i don't remember moans
i remember groans
of disappointment
sometimes i just wasn't what she wanted
both of us reaching
outside ourselves faithfully.

i don't tell her everything
because words are seeds
planted.
there is no telling
who will harvest the crop
you leave behind.
there is no telling where words will blossom
or if they will grow limbs
that shed petals in every wind.

i don't tell her everything

because i don't know where to begin.
because i don't know how to go within
with someone witnessing it
so i'm just sitting here
making idle conversation.

Femmes Dating

We
Who humor
Conversation
For our safety
From men
Who invite themselves to our table.
We who remain polite
Though frustrated
While declining dinner invitations.

We who smile, tired
Of being objects
Of unwanted desire.

We who wear heels
That don't undermine
Our sometimes
Masculine edge
Looking like everyone else
With our
Make-up
Lipstick
Dresses
Fresh manicures
And flowing tresses
Don't
Scream
The message
No
You can't buy us a drink.

dating poets

ambiguity and vagueness
are valuable assets of a good poem
but poems are not conversations
you should have in relationships.
she loves beautiful language
even if she understands nothing said.
she is comfortable never to say anything, literally.
arguing, even when speaking figuratively
there is no alluding telling our truths.
happy- write about the sunshine.
sad- write about the rain.
get this wrong and the sun will cry
or each rain drop will be a smiling kiss
from full lips on the nape of our necks.
'cause we are our poetry
even when we wish
to lose ourselves in it.

I become
A sunflower.
You, Sun.
Rays seduce me
Kneeling and bowing
I worship warmth
Blinded by light
I close my eyes
It's hard to breathe
Inhaling the sky.
Rain showers
Forge a path
In fertile earth
For determined fingers
Reaching
Below
The water table
Claiming the root chakra
As an anchor
Suspended in dance
And drum
Invoking your spirit
Also cum.

already

if god is love
i'm
already an atheist,
i don't believe in chasing or waiting for love
been on my own, so long
i know love will never come, or has already gone
so i gotta believe god is me or god's in me
cause i know god's nowhere out there
already.

so i am, being
all love
all light
no more than the words i write
i have abandoned humanity
sanity
mixing bible scriptures with profanity
already nothing tangible enough to grasp
i seep through her hands
beyond comprehension
rejecting any expectation that might
crush dimensions
i refuse to be status quo, or pretentious
i refuse to be a lie, or a truth relenting
i refuse to be liked or loved at the cost of false
religions
so i lie pliable
and loose
a whore for truth
all ready for the abuse
what will be said?

she says,
"i sure hope you're not one of those poets who
can't speak in clear sentences
who communicates in symbols and analogies
'cause that shit's just too deep for me"
as i wait to speak
already fighting perception
already
trying to be seen behind what she's projecting
already doing my own projecting
what looks like arrogance but is self-acceptance
guarded, trying to reveal what's not protected
stop calling me elitist cause i'm selective
already trying not to be too sensitive
or feel disrespected
already trying to allow the truth
to be whatever it is
not some past or future representative.

i'm
already someone else
i have yet to speak for myself
our first date, first meeting, she doesn't believe me
she tells me all the ways she doesn't need me
i am some collection of poems
she's been reading
some god she's been kneeling before.
instead of saying she's intimidated
she keeps calling me a pimp
and
refusing to be my whore.
she keeps calling me a pimp

and
asking where are my whores.
while wanting me up on a pedestal
she can kneel before.
but i don't want her to be a servant
or worshiper
i just want her
and
i want her to see me.
how can she tell me who i am
when i am me?
part of me wonders
what is the point of speaking?
part of me considers leaving
part of me has stopped believing
part of me has stopped breathing
part of me has stopped seeking
love.

i trust people to be who they are
i explain
avoiding attachment to expectations
i ask fewer questions.
answers never made love safer.
i savor
her
being.
this kind of trust is wiser
freeing.
i learn from her actions
weighed against her intentions
they reveal a pattern
i'll loosely expect her to follow.
the only constant is change.

i trust people to be who they are
allowing them to be
finite and human
catastrophic and peace
breaking, broken and healing
inconsiderate and feeling
and flawed, and infinite, and god
present and lost
but she won't receive
the idea of "self" as deception
snared in external conceptions
turned on
by how keenly i see and reflect her
blindly believing we're deeply connected
reaching for herself and
never touching me.

on wednesday
i wanted to be a dream
a fantasy
a tear exhausted, evaporated and wasted
i wanted to be relieved
hugged
and fucked
and kissed
and called just to say hello
just to breathe
and be answered
visited
worshiped
throned.

on wednesday
i wanted to be a harp
a song hummed lazily
incoherently in the midst of progress
repetitious monotony eluded by new thoughts
dreams and possibilities.

yesterday
i wanted to be a dove
a wing
a cloud
a storm
a star
something above this earth
something that could see the whole picture
someone who could crop a picture
without mourning the space outside of need
what is needed?

i wanted to be the one who knew what was needed.
i needed, need
want, wanted my needs to be met
embraced
and relieved.
i wanted to be healed, and whole
and absent from this transition
growth
tightness lurking in my shoulder blade.
i wanted to be a new conversation
received and igniting
i wanted to be a kiss
a hug
a tongue
a drug
to subdue the pain of being who i really am
me.
where i really am
here.

we brought all our abandonment
save me savior-
crucifying martyr drama
and god complexes
felt a connection
so strong the sex was
yawning
satisfied
at the morning
of new prospects.
silent and wise
it's scary
we can't see ourselves
through the other's eyes.

we
who like to control
each other's perspective
innately become deceptive.
i always want to be who i am
but it's more comfortable in a disguise.
so i just say
thank you
for last night
smiling a shy good bye
when i really want to say
for you
i'd die.
for you
about you
i write.

every time i come to the page

i step off the edge of comprehension
abandon the need to be comprehended
and defensive.
feel that?
just feelings.
just saying what i'm feeling
truth is infinite
and so am i
and so are the lies
that are more comfortable to tell
than telling on myself.
i feel the truth on my soul
but lies are carved in my skin
where they are more tangible in the mirror
than the abstracts of "spirit."
i can't handle them
or grasp time
there's no rewind
they are recorded in my mind
against my will,
i play them for myself
against my will
i play myself for them.
so i can't help but spill
a few.
i didn't mean to lie to you.
do you always tell the truth,
do you always tell?

who am i talking to?
you?
myself?
this paper?

internalized self-hatred?
is this a poem?
or a prayer?
god! why did i tell you i would never fail you?
haven't you ever failed yourself?
i've failed me too
but i still try to be here
there
to be fair
but life is unfair
so you'll still be disappointed
and i'll still be haunted
'cause i put my best foot forward
but life keeps
pushing me back
and i'm not making excuses
i'm just stating facts
and i said all this to say that
whenever i'm human
you make me feel useless.
when all i need is for you to
see my worth even when you're hurt
and know i never mean to hurt
and i never mean to hurt you
just knowing you hurt, hurts too
and it's a two-edged sword
when i know i did the dirt too.
but we both deserve truth and i deserve you
and you deserve to know the truth about you
and us
neither one of us
are perfect.
love,

love means hurting.

just trying to put all this in perspective
the truth is relatively irrelevant.
i was never perfect but i wanted to be.
i thought you wanted me
but i am who i am and not who i wanted to be.
so stop expecting me
to always meet my own high expectations.
let's stop living in futures and pasts
let's stop living in dreams
let's get out of our heads
let's choose another path
let's not let go of each other's hand
let's stop running from the last love we had
and touch each other here
let's teach each other here
let's reach forever here
and now.
let's conquer our fears
and vow
to end all this destruction
to be more trusting
to be more loving
and when i act ugly
can you just
mean mug me?
and when i find my place
will you hug me?
'cause despite my failings
i'm struggling
to love me
as much as i love you.

do you
love me, too?

leave.come back.give me space.stay.

i need you.
i need you to leave me alone
but walk away slow
and keep looking back
to see if i'm longing,
too prideful to call.

i need you.
with no expectations.
but i expect you to leave whenever i say so
and i expect you to be here
without me telling you to
you should just know.
i need you.

i need you to let me be
creation, creator and creating
and free
and words
and alienating
and isolated
and human.
i need you to save me.
i need you to shelter me.
i need you to stand as a buffer
between myself and others,
between who i am and who i wanted to be.
save me from me.
i need you to know the difference
between crying out
and needing to be alone.

i need you to hold me.
i need you to let me go.
i need you to smother me
with your kisses.
i need you to listen.
i need you to be attentive.
i need you to help me make decisions.
i need you to stay out of my business.
i need you to respect my convictions.
i need you to find me
when i'm hiding.
i need you to leave
if you find me writing.
i need you to stay
when i'm on an emotional island.
i need you to leave
before the tide rises.
i need you to stay.
i need you to go away.
i need you here.
and i need you to leave.
and i need you
to let this be.
i need you.
leave. save yourself.
stay. and keep rescuing me.
leave.
i need you.

Sharing

I hear how your day went
In the way you breathe
Before saying hello in the phone.
I feel when you are upset
I feel you, internally speaking to your spirit
Trying to stay positive
Refusing to give up
Trying to put your best foot forward.

Now that you have come out
Your mother says you're lost
And she never should have let you go so far.
She blames herself for "how you are"
But it doesn't stop her from blaming you
And me too
And the "evil Atlanta homosexual" community.

We are silent.
You are pretending to read a magazine at the nook
in my kitchen
I have chosen each song playing
Especially for you
I am cooking us dinner
But I want to feed you in other ways.
This isn't our first date
Or our last.
We are still getting to know ourselves
With each other's self.
You have been down
So I'm trying to anchor you with my peace
While you, thoughtful

Are doing your best not to disturb mine.
So when I ask how is everything
You answer absently, "Fine."
Then resign in a long exhausted sigh.
May I hold your troubles awhile?
Can I anchor you here in time
Ease your mind
Give you pleasing sighs
May I…?

Confronting Pretense

It is late.
I am here.
You are transparent.

Be my sheet of glass.
Let me press my face to your coldness
And breathe deep, warm breaths on your flesh
Then write my name in your moistness
With precise fingertips.

if she doesn't stay
she is contentment
in wanting
in loss.
i'm never absent from the moment.
i will have no regrets.
i hold her every chance i get
tightly, warmly, tenderly, passionately
knowing
all good things come to an end.

butterflies

art
introduced us
you dug my poetry
i loved your smile
how it disappeared
and you followed
spirit
emerged
leading listeners
through thresholds
of other lives
to ancestors
as you drummed.

we discussed
energy
source
how we are
slaves
to its force
writer
poet
singer
drummer
dancer.
somehow i came
to beg you:
identify
as just one.
you answered,
"what religion is god?"

activist
owner
hustler
cultivated
by struggle
insisting
everything fair
isn't equal
willing to die
for your people
conflicted
between
their wants and needs
greed
you concede
capitalist
sweet talk them
into buying
anti-consumerism hypocrisy.

lean, brown, tall
muscular build
sharp jawline
you were masculine
even before
in a dress
now in acceptance
you are something else.

joining hands
interlacing fingers
my palm

kisses yours
as i
mentally speak affirmations
to get anchored
in my own greatness
that i do not worship you
or feel honored
to have your attention.
that i am present
not worrying
about your intentions
or contemplating
how to make you stay.

Prospects

i am a girl who likes girls

not just any girls
witty funny pretty girls
sarcastic condescending silly girls
lesbians
dykes
butches
studs
queers
femmes
aggressives
tombois
the androgynous
and stems.
i like individuals
intellectuals
hustlers and professionals
not afraid to break the silence
with special eating diets
and personal rituals.
i like girls who are so spiritual
they're haunting
penetrating and binding
our souls and minds when
we're cumming.
literally summoning
the moment.
i like girls who be on it
and under it
and above simple shit
moved by the simplest shit
all up in my shit

calling me on my shit
making me better
making me wetter
i said i wouldn't but then i let her.
cause i like them girls who like them girls
who love themselves
and love like there's nothing else
but love.

crushes
dreams
breathe in the seams
holding me
unraveling
i remember to be here
kissing lyrics and dreams
and tears
and fears
away.

what you say
what i say
words bleed the day
and silences restore us during the night.

touching to let go
grasping to be held
somewhere in your absence
and presence
i give myself
and get myself
pieced together
and whole.

Be Boi Swag

She does something different
With rhythm
The way she walks
How she talks
Ain't no heels
Or hip rotations
No nails or make up
None of the customary
Clocking dimensions
But don't get it twisted
People are still paying attention.

With sly glances
Taking in masculine stances
The way she leans when standing
Like picture poses
She's doing something different with clothes and
Something different with prose and
It's flowing
Smooth
She's some other kind of poem
With her own groove.
She's the relativity in blues
Some meditative or melancholy jazz tune
Some DJ that makes the crowd move
Some spirit so consumed by its own truth
It won't be tamed
It's inflamed
And freeing
Laying a path against the grain
By just being.

I hope her ears are ringing
Her spirit is singing
And she's compelled
To smile
Proud
When people stare
At her unquestionable style
Or even do that little church laugh
When she thinks about how
Much I am
In love with her
Be Boi Swag.

She brings to the surface
All my insecurities
Without saying a word.

Without saying a word
I wonder
Then ask
Never in words
Never point blank
Can I
Will I
Measure up?

She holds me
To no standards.
Still I feel inadequate
I've never helped her up the steps
To my pedestal.
Still I worship her.

I was compelled to speak to her
Now I want to
Forget
Reflex.
I want to forget
She's a threat
To the hard foundation I built.
I want to forget
Eyes like chisels
Chipping away
Weakening it.
I want to forget.

i get her

i loved her with a hungry contemplation
fed by information
without expectation.
i am piecing her together.
how do you love someone you do not know?
how do you know?

i push her around in my mental rolodex
turn pages of conversations
ask questions
to give her depth.
i've gotten so good i show her, herself
it pleases her
that i get her
it pleases me
that i get her
all to myself.

the prospect

what did we have really?
too many things in common, not to be friends
enough attraction to be lovers?
we had lived, made mistakes.
we were too old for silly shit.
we'd heard and told enough lies
to know it was time
to just get out with the truth
on with the living
on with the judgments
adding and subtracting
examining each other.
did either of us add up
within the equations of ourselves?
were we equals?
fractions?
wholes?

infinite, i
don't always make sense to myself
so i try to be precise and clear for everyone else.
sometimes this level of honesty has helped
others lead me to my own truth.
so i thought about what i said
said what i thought
felt it
meant it.
if lying occurred to me-
i examined why i wanted to lie
overcame those fears
refused my ego any satisfaction

forced myself to tell the truth.
i am doing my best not to be misunderstood
not even by myself.
which means sometimes i'm making annotations
corrections and giving references
to explain
actions and conversations past and present.
which means
sometimes i make myself a liar
a hypocrite.
i don't want to be perceived
greater or less than i am
nor do i want to be crowded into a box.
i wanted her to see me, feel me, want me
just me.
even though i hadn't figured out
whether I wanted her.
i had dated too long to be excited
i was hopeful
open
seriously considering the possibility of an us.
i wanted us to have all the facts
when deciding if we wanted to be together.

out with it!
no one is perfect!
i wanted to be a truth with no holes.
when flipped or shaken i still wanted to make sense
and be dependable.
so when, or if
she ever needed a strong foundation
i'd be a brick wall

if ever too high in the clouds or lost at sea
i wanted to be an anchor
an island
a light house.

still, she lied to me
even though we bonded on being single
'cause we were tired of shit not adding up
'cause we refused to settle.
she played all the games we agreed we hated.
she lied to me.
things didn't add up.
still i was patient
gave her the benefit of doubt
in hopes that if ever she thought i was lying
or i hadn't examined all the facts
and was somehow lying
to her and myself, she would be patient too.
'cause i wanted to be something other
than a skeptic
something other than disappointed
something other than hurt
something other than judge and jury.
i didn't want to render another verdict
or shut anyone else out
in courting, both sides serve the sentences.
i was tired of pretending
being hurt felt any better than being guilty.
i was tired of being defensive
tired of being self-righteous
as if i'd never done anything offensive.
i wanted to be something other
than all my past experiences

molding yet another experience.
in obedience to my commitment to be present
i waited, to be sure
hoping she wasn't lying
even when experience shouted
"her behavior fits the pattern of a liar!"

human,
i was careful not to scream outright "liar!"
cause maybe i just didn't understand.
plus, we were more than acquaintances
more than friends
not committed lovers
something other.
so i did the math orally before her.
initially asking, "what am i missing?"
each time there was no solution.
i'd point out "a variable is missing."
when i was convinced
she was too intelligent not to see the voids
and was refusing to acknowledge them
i challenged her,
"what are you afraid of?"
'cause i think lying is about fear,
about covering up inadequacy,
and maybe a fear of rejection.
i assured her, i was there.
then i gave her some rope
to pull herself up
and she did
better than that
she climbed an old tree with several mature

branches
then hung herself.

compelled to stare

a radiant sun even in the
shadows of intimate lighting
her arrival is an unannounced
event
bowing her head and eyes
humbly, feline
her locs undulating in the wind,
a flag of beauty
a pageant, without
accompaniment or applause
she does not play to the crowd
observed
but not observant
it is special to catch her eye
she steps purposeful
chin high
displaying how deities glide
among the clouds
from her soul she greets,
invites, welcomes and smiles
her teeth
and the whites of her eyes
are light liquefied
immersing the room
making the repetitive seem
brand new.

Femme Theory

All femme lesbians
Are bisexuals
Or closeted heterosexuals.
No matter what they say.
No matter what I said
She feared me
Leaving her
For a man.

friends
becoming lovers
becoming other
saying no hard feelings
healing
maybe we further wound
burn a bridge or two
and stay cross.
can we be cordial?
will we casually fuck?
or delete and block
or secretly stalk
or be secretly stalked?
will we speak
when we run into each other in the streets?
in my absence
will you still be a friend to me?
i don't want to talk about you
are you discussing me?

Deeper Than You Think
(Ode to the Drag Kings)

Dressed, reared and marveled by the gods
Envied by the elite
I bleed Ichor
I am she
The Love Goddess
Aphrodite
Pay homage to my pearl
Emerged from the sea
Golden palms and golden feet
I am
Deeper than you
Deeper than you think.

Now you have known valleys and
You have sailed seas, but not as
Deep as me
I weave light from darkness
Guide, when you can't see
Sun of signs Leo Fire
This Lioness is your queen
King if that's what you desire
Though I know bowing alone
Could never please you, Sire
It's gonna take more than good sex
To swallow that hollowed out emptiness
See cause
I know you're lonely
But that's only
Until you hold me
Until you know me

Then I'll show you
That I know you
Better than my words can flow truth
And you'll know too
When I hold you
I am
Deeper than you think.

You want someone
Not impressed with gems and stones
But has a mind of her own
You demand another ruler
To share your throne
Not to mention
You'll refuse a woman attention
If she is pretentious
Self-righteous or judgmental
Can't speak without curse words
In every sentence
Can't express herself in dimensions
Like I can
On every word I stand
Or say nothing at all
Because some issues are far too small
And I refuse to crawl
Or brawl on suspicions
She always wants to talk
But I, I can listen
I know when to be quiet
And just enjoy the silence
Are you feeling me
We could be
Totally

In sync.
I Am
Deeper than you think.

Some call it intuition
I hear your soul's admissions
You'd die for your convictions
Not intimidated by opposition
Sometimes your words seem vicious
But you've learned to be defensive
From a hard background
That guides your decisions
You refuse to surrender
You're aggressive
You're really ambitious
And you'd have to be
Under the weight of your mission.
Your eyes divulge
Such immense feelings
I can imagine what you've seen
Pain, you never have to speak
Love,
I
Am
Deeper than you
Think.
 Between calculated thoughtful refrains
We discussed the word, and I AM's name
When I discovered
I believe what you believe
Lover
You are my Adam
But please

Don't call me Eve
I am better informed than she
No serpent could undermine me
Cultivated in a harsh reality.
There is not room to be naive
Gone is my innocence
And I'm not pretentious
All I am
Is I am
Who is in me.
Who is me?
I am the eye of the tornado
Surrounded by chaos
Centered in peace
Just like life
Both bitter and sweet
I
Am
Deeper than you think.

I understand that
Sometimes you just need silence
Not my crying
Not my intrusive prying
Or cursing the world
For not sympathizing
All the while never realizing
I only dug a deeper hole
When all you needed was to know
I am more than a brown valley
To exhaust your sorrows
All that I am
I became for you to borrow

For however long you're weak
I can be your retreat
Claim your peace
I am
Deeper than you think.

More than a woman, I am an artist
Creating and secreting confidence
You can call me
Venus
Just a little smaller than the earth
I could be your world
Rotating from west to east
I could nurture your seeds
I'll be
The sun, the moon, the trees
I'll be the grass, and even the breeze
With my arms out-stretched
I'll swell in your flesh
Find your strength and resurrect it
Be that pride-filled breath
That inflates your chest
Make you throw your shoulders back and
Project your best
Without me, you can't experience yourself
Never see the spring
Where you profess
What it is you were born to manifest
I am so much of you
And you are so much of myself
I have your rib
We were made of one flesh
And for us to be in love is

And for us to be in love is
And for us to be in love is
Instinct
I am
Deeper than you think.

Breaking Up

moving in with lovers

dating
you welcomed faults
idiosyncrasies
said inconveniences were
acts of love
and even when painful
gave you unexpected
satisfaction.

you insisted i
make myself at home
outside of your bedroom too
inviting me into your kitchen
your tub
your office
into the yard to help prune roses
explaining it was no home
when i was away.

i let go of my place.

moving me in
you resented anything
you deemed unnecessary.
i kept many bags packed
stored in the basement
lived as if in transition
out of boxes labeled
with broken promises
"kitchen"
"living room"

"office."

we fought
over pieces of myself
you wanted to trash.
i had better style
you openly envied.
you were a hoarder
you openly admitted.
still, i made myself small
for you
until i disappeared.

there is love
even in the breaking
that won't be mistaken
as a basis for staying.
we are just
sorting through
our lives and things
brought here
bought here
"you can have this"
"you keep that"
"you're the only one who uses it."

what about mutual friends?

i mourn the good parts of her
that are not tangible
and spread over our space
to negotiate
keeping.
i dread tomorrow
after this shared space is clear.
as if we were never here.
anchored and absent
reimagining life
without her.

if apologies are selfish
how do i get near you
tell you i fear you?
and this destructive behavior
is me fighting
feeling
being
here.

if it is selfish to call you
to want you
after you've gone
after we've agreed to move on
after you've gotten tired of me letting go
'cause i was too afraid to hold on
you might have actually appreciated
knowing i was intimidated.
but i think it's too late and
now you don't trust me enough to feel me.
what should i do with all these feelings?
wondering
if this moment is free
if you'd be willing to hear me?

you said my silence
made you feel like i didn't like you.
i remember saying
you're amazing
and didn't we agree
we were what the other had been anticipating?
didn't we say we were the consolation for all the
waiting?
now i regret i am so shy and

silence
is me hiding
i've been so thoroughly hurt
love is frightening.

i know
this apology is selfish.
even if you would listen
i can't promise
who i've become
would be okay dying
afraid of being left in the future
i can't grasp the moment.
my journey to love is becoming
a different woman
without a space conducive
to evolving.
and who has that kind of patience?
how can i ask you to come back
for waiting?

i put peace and light between us
with an email
instructing her
"please don't contact me to explain yourself."
still she called
but i hung up to save myself
blocking emails, messages, texts
even IM's
'cause she spoke bullshit from her diaphragm.
her voice tone, a moan
soft enough to be a whisper
deep enough to be her fingers on your drum.
somehow when she spoke she sung.
that's why i
refuse to hear her speak
her voice makes me weak.
i couldn't even hear her
breathe, or pause, or sigh
she was some type of stud who probably never
would
but i
wanted her so much
i just might cry
and listen
to her BS
ignoring myself.

i'd love to talk
wanted to talk even when i didn't want to talk.
i wanted her
i wanted her to embrace me in denial
wanted her to say it was all in my mind
that she was absent

wanted her to call my loneliness while she was here
some other thing.
maybe i was the one disconnected
from myself
but my spirit wouldn't accept that.

so i hung up
wanting.
i wanted her to give me reasons
to help my fear seem irrational.
i wanted her to help me deny my intuition
i wanted her
i wanted her
more than i wanted to be right
or writing
or words
or piecing together this fucking poem
missing her.
i was always missing her.
still
i wanted palms connected
fingers interlaced on long walks
and talks about goals, and dreams or whatever other
things.
i wanted to hear her stories.
i wanted to tell her mine.
i wanted the comfortable silence
interwoven in the space of rituals
performed out of necessity.
i wanted the density of her presence so strong
we were connected and i was touched
even when she was gone.
i wanted to sleep in the curl of her arm.

i wanted her
but she was
unavailable.

Platonic Toxic Love

I remind myself we're friends
When I'm emotionally exhausted
Drawing lines in the sand
Determining what I can give
And what I can accept.
After you've already volunteered
More than I ever asked
Needed or wanted from you
After you are feeling used
After I've refused
To answer questions meant to wound.

I ask myself
What is wrong with someone loving me too much?
Bracing myself to stay
Because I always remember being abandoned.
I've got a list of god-assigned blood ones
Who never loved me.
You always encourage my dreams
In my absence
You speak favorably of me.
When I declare war
You are poised on the front line
To go down with me.
I'm trying to forget all the times you asked
If you could go down on me
Hoping your feelings will pass.
Friends
Are the only family I have.
Friends are the only family we get to choose.
I choose you.

But if we emotionally abuse each other too
If we guilt trip and bruise each other too
If we don't own and address our issues
Where is our refuge?
It hurts me to hurt you
With the truth
I love you
But I'm not in love with you
Friend.

why are you calling me?
the question is an interrogation
a threat
another slap in the face
another way to crush my already fragile spirit.
it may not be her intent
but it is her way
and whatever the intent
i am crushed
reminded why i shouldn't have called.
the power switches
i feel the distance
and the denial of myself
led by my heart
my want of her.
this moment trains me
not to be true to instinct
or passion
but stand erect
never looking back
with my head leading
and my heart will follow
or suffer.
maybe it will suffer after all.

Marked Urgent

I wanted to tell you something
Needed to tell you something
Needed to say it more than breathing.
Held my breath waiting, anticipating
Your reaction
Void of action
More than being
Started feeling
Like maybe that was telling me something.
And I heard what I wanted to say
Heard what I needed to hear
Would have ignored it
If you were here
Listening.
If I was just speaking
I would have missed the necessity
I was seeking
Outside
Your absence out there
Closed me in
Embraced in tears
Cocoons of youth, wisdom too
Sour and blue
Purple and true
Royally new
Divinely enlightened I recognized too
That letter
Was mistakenly addressed to you.
Maybe this was a lesson for more than one
But are you two?
Are you too

Needing to hear this message?

note to self
she confirms all my fears
never should have come here
outside myself.
to ease the pain
i swallow myself
now just a shell
a representative
to keep up appearances
smiling.
feelings are irrelevant
burdens fools weigh heavier
than facts.

Ties That Bind

She wasn't *being* abrasive
She *is* abrasive.
With her
Everything is black and white.
I had too many gray areas
For her to feel secure.
She needed boxes
To keep me locked in.
But I wanted to be free.
So she let me be.

ME

If you, love ME
Love ME
Love ME

If you, love ME
Love ME
Love ME

ME
Not who you wanted me to be
Not who you expected me to be.
Not all your past hurts projected on me
Not a taller or smaller me
Not if I was a baller me
Not a brighter lighter me
Or a better job title me.
ME.
The fighter ME
I'm a writer ME
A fire lighter powder keg igniter ME
I'm a busy bee
A summer breeze
Tired feet laying paths
Over a quarter century
On the road an old soul
All soul
Leaving footprints carved in stone
Tired of walking alone
ME.
Baby, I adore YOU
And ME

Share this journey with ME
But don't threaten to leave ME
Just leave
Cause if you Love ME
Love ME
Love ME
Love ME.

Stop wishing I'd be like everyone else me
Or more like yourself me
Stop calling ME pessimistic me
I'm just a realist ME
Aware ME
Up on my global affairs ME
Picking her poison ME
Refusing to take orders ME
Or take what's given to ME.
Believe none of what you've heard
And half of what you've seen
Constantly evolving ME
Not the past me
Not searching for my other half me
I'm a whole ME
Love to make you laugh ME
So if you'll have ME
Love ME
Love ME
Love ME.

I won't be waiting
For your family to embrace ME
Or your friends to celebrate ME
Even if no one appreciates ME

I'll be ME.
Not a prettier me
Or a wittier high sadiddier me
Not a giddier me
Or a fitter me,
ME.
Not the "if I understood you better" me
But the go getter ME
The introspective ME
A reflective poetic protective ME
The neglectful, sincerely apologetic ME
The "I didn't know that would hurt you" ME
The sometimes inconsiderate
Always trying to be a considerate ME
The best intentions ME
Striving to be a better ME
The regretfully forgetful ME
The "I didn't get it" ME
"Oh, now I get it" ME
"Now you gone get it" ME.
Not some fantasy
Or bandage for your insecurities
Or an excuse for your inadequacies.
I'm no dramatic tragedy
I'm a passionate ME
With a few idiosyncrasies
Who won't pretend to be any other me
Cause if you Love ME
Love ME
Love ME
Love ME

ME.

Not saint, sinner, worshipper or deity
Just connected connecting connection
Divine Energy
Whatever the moment calls ME to be
Whatever the moment reveals in ME
Whatever life is dealing ME
I'm feeling ME
The knowing and seeking ME
The naive subject and all-knowing queen
The "sometimes ego gets the best of" ME
Pain taught humility
Overstanding lessons given to ME
Wisdom resonates within ME
Speaking emphatically
If you
Loved
ME,
You'd
Love
ME.
Love ME
Love ME
Love ME.

ME.
Not who I struggle to be
Not all the masks
I juggle to please.
Stop judging ME
Start trusting ME
And Love ME for ME
Not the younger me
Not the slimmer trimmer me

Not the physically athletic
Or beautifully aesthetic me
Or when I'm older
"Then I'll see what you really mean" me.
No
ME
Right now
Literally and metaphorically
Spiritually and religiously
In this moment
Wherever I am
Whatever I be
However I am
Whomever I be,
ME.
If you Love ME
Love ME
Love ME
Love ME
Love
ME.

Rebound Poems

Grateful

Thank you, God
For loving me
When I could not or would not love myself.
When I wanted to go back
But there was no place to stay.
When I wanted to hold on
But they were cacti.
When I was willing to change
But I was forced to be myself.
When I just didn't want to be alone
You showed me freedom
I'd never known.
Now I dread relationships
I'm comfortable alone.

in the mean time
it's all love
trying
to find peace
waiting
searching
being
free
praying
for an anchor.
cursing self
for not just sailing
arms open wide
spine surfing tide
soul embracing
sky
hypnotized.

when this heart breaks
it just consumes
and consumes my soul, too.
chewed
chewing gum
never in pieces always one
whole piece ground between teeth
gathering minced meat
and other particles
all becoming part of a
baptismal spit.
rebirth.
walked on.
kicked.
ignored.
breaded in earth
served
when swallowing air gets mundane
hurting others loses taste.
biting tongue.
how does one
maintain distance?
incapable of being numb.
passions grown
too much to chew on
so my peace is mixed
with a little blood.

a live band's drumming
is a soundtrack
for wandering.
lost in my head
surrounded by trees
on my back
in a plush bed of grass
intoxicated,
by steel blue skies
stinging eyes
soothing soul.
for a moment
i am not lonely.
i am whole.
tears make streams
to my ears
christening the beginning
of healing
and becoming a new being.
for a moment
i'm so wholeheartedly connected
i forget this self, this shell
and your chi and dreams
release their hold on me.
and i let go of us
and you
and you
embracing the beauty and blessing of today
looking forward
to more tomorrows.

I compare every woman to you
Have your face
Etched in my mind.
Every time someone talks about breaking up
Or divorce
I miss you.
Start wondering if there is such a thing
As forever love
Or unconditional
It's been forever, Love
Since we broke up
But you are
Still
Carved in my heart.
I remember
The tone of your voice
How your eyes slim
And your cheeks brighten
When you laugh and smile
How you lean in to listen
How you muffle your own cries
While trusting me to see you vulnerable
Swallowing disappointment.
I am hurting now
At the thought of your sadness
Hoping you're happy.

I remember you
Beautiful
Even when angry
And callous.
I remember you whole
Even when broken.

I remember you perfect
Even though I left you
For all your exquisite imperfections.

Even in the end
She instructs
Never call me if we break up.
I don't want to be reshelved.
I never want to be friends with exes.
Just let it end.
Let me go.
I don't want to be one of those bitches
You cling to.

Often she says she knows
I feel like I'm being controlled
But that is not who she is
Or what she wants.
I leave to breathe.
There are so many rules.
I'm suffocating.

I miss her
But I don't call or text
Even though I'm usually friends
With my ex.

When I run into her
I'm not friendly.
In fact, I try to be cold
'Cause even in the end
I'm still submitting to her control.

on the rebound yah bastids

i was never afraid to admit it
just hadn't occurred it was true
and frankly
i was offended everyone kept telling me
"slow down
you are on the rebound."
my famous response
"contrary to popular opinion
i am not rebounding
because i have not missed my shot."

the transition was wonderful
until i stopped moving
and people started wanting to connect
but i was too slippery to hold on to
too fluid to hold in hands, or embrace.
melting into myself
i could not be present
i could not be called or remembered
i could not be expected, or waited on
because sometimes i was cumming and not coming
sometimes i was cumming and not there
sometimes i was going, but never coming back.
sometimes i was going and coming
but could not differentiate between them
just moving
got tah, got tah keep moving.

i feel the rhythm of this obsidian man
with a fro so big, nappy and beautiful
it is his own atmosphere.

he thunders and reigns the corner in fitted clothes
like an old seventies b movie
but he moves and grooves
pulsating with his own virility
thin as a rail
he exudes so much strength
it's hard to tell he isn't a running back.
a-shirt and bellbottom denims cling to every muscle
writhing under his flesh
with each strike of his drum.
ashy lips keep rhythm better than the heart itself
tapping it out like his life depends on it.
"got tah, got tah keep moving" he wails.
i'm afraid if i stand too long, listening
i'll be paralyzed here.

see, i could say
i don't miss the scent of your body
clean or funky
in my sheets, on my lips and cheeks.
see, i could say
i don't miss waking up to you so much
sometimes i don't want to wake up
and maybe all this transition sex
hasn't been just about the transition sex
(great as that shit is)
maybe it's about fucking until i am too exhausted
to get up and come find you
too exhausted to hurt
or cry
or wonder where you are.
maybe all the transition sex
was less about the night

but more about avoiding the loneliness of mornings.

spoon in hand
patting between palm and knee
he beats out this desperate rhythm for me.
today i gotta little change for his ass
cause i feel the pain of all things unimagined
us worse than strangers
we're choosing to be nothing to each other.
i could dwell forever
on how i used to love her
but i
got tah got tah keep moving.

i love the way your cheek creases
when you smile
the way your eyes squint when you're angry
or really listening
the way you crumble into yourself
when you laugh.
i love when you are out of breath
enjoying yourself
and tell me
it's the way i make you laugh
that makes you love me.
when i am honest about it all
it wasn't all that bad
was it?
got tah, got tah, keep moving.

he plays a beat so desperate

i want to slump down on the dirty curb
and press my back against the piss-stained wall.
this shit ain't for me at all
this song
is for his own disenfranchisement.
he's staring off into space
some other place.
i'm wishing for a familiar space
your familiar face.
wishing i wasn't packed shit cakes
in this lunch bag life
i've been handed.
wishing i didn't feel like i was on another planet.

love?

I remember things
Better than they were.
I say, "I feel so alone, now."
As if you were ever here
You were always leaving
You were always reading
Into things.
You never looked at me.
You were always
Judging
And I was always guilty.

not glass
i cannot be broken
just hopeless.
went out
avoiding loneliness.
found god
in a reggae bar.
got the holy ghost
danced
freeing
spirit
from flesh
until i was exhausted
enough to rest.

your voice is higher than i remember
you're more direct than i recollect.
were you always this insensitive?
i never realized you were cruel
and selfish too.
i was successful
at believing what i was projecting
you went along enough to be deceptive
and i was
always dodging you.
i lived in a dream.
trying to please you
trying to heal too
while not acknowledging wounds
i was always coming for you
abandoning myself.
running
running
from myself.

now, i'm standing still
you have been anchored oceans away
and i don't like the island you are on after all.
did i ever?
but it would be cool to visit
and leave before the tide rises.
it would be cool to visit
and leave before the sun sets.
it would be cool to visit
but leave before the sun peaks

all i've wanted
is to be intertwined in the stars with you

then i realized i didn't like heights
or reaching
or maybe you were not as high as i thought.
maybe i have grown beyond worshiping you
or
you have found a new pedestal.
maybe today is what it is
and yesterday was then.

In the Absence of Love
The dark holes in the sky
Are not occupied by stars
Anxiously awaiting a little light
For their moment to shine.

The dark holes are empty expanses
In a spider-less web
Hungrily waiting to devour dreams before first light
'Cause
There are darker blues than midnight.

A Love Poem In Your Absence

For the people who break our hearts
Then smile
And laugh
Who call only to talk about themselves
Probably, never noticing at all.

For the people who break our hearts and call
Wanting to be cool and talk
About nothing at all
Pinching on our silence
Asking why we're so quiet
Trying
To avoid feeling the void by filling the void
We've been attempting to ignore.
All I can talk about is how you've broken my heart
You don't want to hear that any more
So you ask what's new with me
As if you never knew me
Every day is the same even though people change
I'm still in pain now
All I can think about is how
'Cause all I feel is
Space
Between us
Space.

For the people who attempt to soothe
Spiritual wounds
With "But, we are still friends
And "I will always love you."
Dishonoring trust
Jabbing at our openness

By telling us all the reasons they do not love us
The way they begged us to
The way they promised you.

After we have already crossed that bridge
And those planks
Linking then and now
Between friends and lovers
Have crumbled into pieces of puzzles
So jarred and frayed
They don't even recognize each other
In the void between two ends of the universe
Where we once were
Who we once were.

I told you not to come over here!
Didn't I?
You almost didn't make it
Carrying the weight of my fear
I begged you to stay where you were
You pushed, aggressive and reckless as always
Saying you needed me
Making your need of me
My own personal responsibility
You demanded I love you and gave yourself to me
Saying life was about change and love
I felt things were changing Love
So I armed myself in ambiguity and absence
Every time you reached I was detachment
Still your bravery
Was so amazing and the shit you were saying
I pretended not to hear you
Out there wounded and calling

I pretended not to fear you
Removing your armor
We both knew I was stalling
Looking over the edge
Contemplating
Falling.

Reaching for my hand
You said no matter how we land
We'll always be friends
That was our pact
Then I didn't know friendship
Would pale in comparison
Then I was comparing what I had to a place I'd
never been
Then you promised to be there for me
But you're not here.
Where is there?

After you showed up so much at my door
I opened
You came in
Thrashing around
I felt things breaking,
Assumed you were just careless
Moving fragile things
And I trusted you more than I loved fragile things
Priceless things
Trusted you to stay
'Cause you moved so much of your stuff in
You brought all of your baggage
But I'm no airline
So I didn't weigh and charge you per bag

I just kept finding space
Knowing I could fly
No matter how heavy things got
Taking off, flying, I am a star
Too far to catch in this lifetime
So I thought our love was divine
Infinite as the expanse
You filled space
Made my universe seem cozy and safe
Even when unpredictable
You were the ruler and I followed
Feeling protected
Though neglected
I knew we would figure it out.

Abandoned, I
Regret
Allowing you to rearrange things
And throw things away I felt were important
While I was out, falling.
Then I didn't mention it
'Cause I've learned you get new things
Sometimes better things when you let go.
You let go
For new things
Was she a better thing, a better me?
I'm holding on
Because I'm open
You are in
All of your stuff is here
And I told you not to come
Because this dwelling space is permanent.
Even when you're gone

I feel it's your home
I feel so alone.
And you've left so much here
Broke so many fragile priceless things.
I'm too traumatized
To be open
Resolved hopelessness.
I told you I was afraid
Still you scared me and scarred me
Then left
I don't want to seriously entertain anyone else
And I've
Never been one to fuck guests.

Relating

seeking

tired of talking about love
fantasizing
romanticizing
love.
i don't want to write another love poem
read another love poem
be another love poem.

i don't want to discuss how disappointed i am
with the prospects
or how tired i am of the process.

i want to write about accidental meditations
spiritual awakenings
from the dry parts of the ocean's floor.

i want to hold hands on the shore
swallow the horizon
beneath your eyelids
and kiss sorrow away for the last time.
i want the wind to kiss our limbs
and the waves to sing a hymn
we'll inhale and breathe back in bits
of immense darkness
private pleas
cropped between
thighs, bellies
and flailing knees
quelling needs.

i want to write about

a few million great conversations
lingering sexual frustration
reaching a crescendo every other day and
staring at the ceiling
in arms, just thinking
and silence leaking
spilling peaceful
into
pilots
lit
ignited
and we're fire.
flying.

i want to write about
it being uncommon
sharing so many things in common
and being so different
it's interesting.

i want to laugh 'til the sun rises
cry 'til the sun sets
exhausted and wet
from kisses.

i want to remember who i was before i was
expected
i want to be fully accepted
and fully accepting
undulating like an african drum projecting.
i want to write about life unrestricted
i want to write about moments not taken for granted
and total forgiveness

of others and self.
i want to write about love
and nothing else.

with you
i try not to submit
or subject you to small mindedness
by pushing myself
to see beyond each moment
to the bigger picture.

with you
i'm sincerely reading and applying scripture
and any other relationship literature
because we don't have a good family history
still establishing our support systems
and this moment in time
is all about being individuals.
when i want to be with you.
i want to be all of myself
with you.
i don't want to become anyone else
with you.
i want to become more of myself
with you.

with you
i'm trying to be forgiving
without becoming a doormat or resentful.
i'm trying to be loving
making you a priority without becoming fixated
i'm trying to be dependable and unchanging
without becoming complacent.
with you
i'm trying to be supportive without enabling.
with you
i'm trying to support your believing

your freedom
your weaning from a cycle of devastation.
with you
i am freely giving
i am passionately living.
i am freely trusting.
with you
i am not destructive.
with you
there will be no judgement.
with you
i'm listening with intuition
trying to respond with wisdom.
with you
i am only open to debating
no blaming or shaming.
any criticism will be constructive.
even when things get ugly
and you're speaking destructive
i will remind myself i love you.

with you
i've decided to share
the rest of my life journey.
no matter what happens
i'm choosing not to see you strange
nor treat you like a stranger.
with you
i haven't decided if i'm saying
i'm willing to live in estrangement.

with you
i don't seek to be understood

just appreciated
given the benefit of doubt
and not underestimated.
with you
i'm striving to be less complicated
more facilitating.
with you
i'm envisioning your dreams
without suffocating
you
beneath your own abandoned expectations.

Femme Privilege

I forgot I was gay
Thought I'd already done all my coming out
My whole family knew, the community too
Then you picked me up from work
And everyone started to treat me differently.

I'd forgotten I was gay
Until you came to talk to the mechanic
And he felt threatened.
Until people stared us down in malls and grocery
stores
Until women started walking back out the restroom
To make sure they'd walked in the right one.
Until people started apologizing for mistaking you
for a sir
Until you excused the mistake saying,
"It's cool 'cause, that's the look I'm going for."

I forgot I was gay
Until you wanted to kiss me good night in front of
my place.
Until you wanted to hold my hand in public.
Until you wanted to show and tell everyone you
loved me.
Until we were sitting over a candlelit dinner
And the waitress was stammering over the daily
specials.
Until I was explaining to my straight friends
Why I would date a woman who was masculine
But not a man.
Until men started asking me why I wanted you

If I didn't want them.
Until the man in the store wanted to fight you
Claiming it was for me, but I didn't know him.

I forgot being gay is different
Until I started being afraid for your safety.
Until I started using my appearance to get us in.
Until I was sometimes dealing with my shame
Dealing with my rage.
Until I understood why you are so paranoid and
afraid.
Until I understood why you are so easily angered
And ready to go there
Until you led me there
And left me
Until I was accepting
As long as we are together
I will be coming out
Forever.

Domestic War

I have been trying to figure out
What to do with this silence
Buzzing between us.
Where words fly like gunfire
Exchanged across a battlefield
And anxious bodies lay in trenches
Fingers on the triggers
Aiming
Aiming.
No one wants to get hit
No one wants it to end here
But we desire more than survival.
Running across the field
Is suicidal.
We both want what's on the other side.
So we try
To bridge gaps
With denial
Dreams
And good intentions.

Ebb and Flow

When her words tickle me
I'm high pitch
Quick speech and labored breathing
Staggering
Happily back to articulation.

When her wit stings
My laughter is a bitter inflection
Sound echoing in flesh like shards of glass
Against spirit
Recalibrating balance
I am a dull chime
Signaling an ineffective meditation
Hummed out of ritual
Hoping for peace.

When I am heard
Our conversations are acoustic
A capella harmony
When I am understood
There is this beautiful syncopation
We are a choir
An audience
Singers of a song rehearsed
Until perfectly delivered
So it no longer requires repetition
Freeing us
To learn
New lessons.

When she yells at me

I become deaf
A fragile whining moan
A strong vent bellowing in defense
Confused by the change of rhythm.

When she moans in rhythm
I am committed to trying new notes
I am a falsetto
A baritone
And soprano
I am a bass and drum
When her palm hits my ass
We call and answer
Whole
Our spirits speak in telepathy
Make me audile
Flush flesh
Broken breaths
And sighs
Of quiet satisfaction.

The Lesson

She says,
"If you leave make sure the next one is a step up."
She is always pointing out how much better she is.
She's always judging.
One of our problems
She determines people's value
By what they own and how much they earn
Or their job title.
She is constantly pointing out who is worthless
And who I should not love or befriend
Based on their usefulness.
She thinks I'm foolish
For choosing
To love based on feelings, spirit and connection.
She's more strategic
Every relationship she has
Is part of a larger plan
I'm no exception.
Though I don't understand how I fit in.

Still she teaches me how much patience I have
She teaches me how much I have grown
She teaches me I am not vindictive
She teaches me not to speak
To people who aren't listening
And not to explain if they are dismissive.

She reminds me of my mother
Who raised me to be a small burden
She sees love as a responsibility.
Pencils me in her schedule.

She reminds me to shine
With all of her darkness.

Out of the blue
Every once in a while
She offers
Maybe you need a blue-collar lover.
Someone who will love your southern girl charm.
Someone who will love home-cooked meals.
Someone who won't ask your credit score.
Or how much is in your 401K.
Someone who won't ask how much you make
Or how much you have in a bank.
Someone who will throw you a little change.
Someone with no real goals
But to work their fingers to the bone
Building you a home.
Someone who will make you her world.
Someone who hides
From the realities of life
Between your legs.

She teaches me who I am
By accusing me of all the things I am not.
She teaches me how far I'll go
By pushing me
Too far.
I've stopped feeling guilty about saying no.
She teaches me how to love myself
Unconditionally
By loving herself even when wrong.
She laughs
When it's pointed out she's being condescending

Says telling the truth isn't verbally abusive.
Says she isn't selfish but self-loving.
Feels it's ok to mistreat people
If she's having a bad day.

She teaches me not to abandon myself
For her
Or for friends who abandon me for staying with her.
She shows me how a person can be absent
Sitting right beside me.
She teaches me what commitment means.
I know she will stay and hurt me
As long as I'm willing to be wounded to learn.
She teaches me to find my voice.
She teaches me to speak my piece.
She teaches me
To make sure there is a clear understanding
About what I'm asking or what I need
By all the times she's taken advantage.
Adding, I only have myself to blame.
She teaches me who my family is
By being here
When they are not.
She teaches me how I love my friends
When I tell her, show her my truth
But don't share myself fully with them.
She teaches who I am
When she is here
And I am not.
She teaches me to embrace my imperfections
By pointing them out

By holding grudges
And trying to punish me
With head games or silence
Or verbal attacks.
She teaches me to laugh in the eye of a storm
When I really want to tase her.
She reminds me
God is in control
Because I prayed for her.

I Came For You, Love

I walked here
From the Serengeti, barefoot.
I climbed mountains
Every step tested my grasp
My intentions
And my ability to pull my own weight.

Birds are unreliable
When you don't have wings.
I abandoned anchors
Walked on water
Strengthening my devotion.
Faith was, is
Believing
Despite my past
I am perfect
For someone
For you.

I thank God
For wounds.
Tending them taught me compassion.

I thank God
For allowing me to inflict pain
On myself and others.
Now I am considerate
Deliberate
With my words
Hands, feet, spirit, heart and energy.
Once anchored in something that felt like regret

Guilt
But really was a girl used to being treated small
Playing small
Making room for herself
Acknowledging her power
Accepting her divinity
Empowered to harness her energy, consciously
And forgive
Others
And Self.
That's humility
Freedom
And mercy
Worthy of salvation
All of us are entitled to love.
But dysfunction-
Dysfunction teaches us
Love must be deserved
Or earned.
It took me years to learn
Love is infinitely spiritual
And we are all
Divine manifestations
Of our creator.
Sanctified to make it
Physical
Tangible
Sacred.

It Was Her

She was afraid
Someone would take me away
But everything I ever wanted in a woman
It was her.

She was clocking every move
Had me on house arrest too.
And then there were interrogations
Checking my cell phone
Scrutinizing text conversations.
I kept thinking eventually she would get it
I must care
Or I wouldn't be there.

Still
She felt threatened by everyone else.
I was always defending myself
And explaining who she was.
For me, she was love.
I told her I chose her.
She told me to choose myself.
I never understood what that meant.

I needed her
Breathed her
Wanted to be so close
Sometimes I wanted to be her.
I always wanted to be there
She never had to wonder
Or ask me to stay

If anything was pushing me
away
It was her.

She breaks me
Open
Nervous
Hopeful
She will not abandon what she finds.
Fingernails to spine
Hands secure my behind
Spirit and flesh aligned.
We grind.
Mentally intertwining
Emotionally unwinding
Freedom we're finding
In the binding.
We grind.
Moving against the relentlessness of time
We grind
We grind.

After years
Broken
I am healing
I am open
Overflowing
Willing
Knowing
Each piece
Is safe with her.
Waiting for her
Escaping her
Saving her
Braving her
Every morsel
Guarded in a sacred place.

I forgive her
For throwing my truth in my face.
We are beyond our fears
Beyond our self-hate, hate
Our dwelling is a safe space.

With a sincere appreciation of time
Our future is sublime
Our past behind.
Aging, evolving
We try
To pin and wrestle time
Kissing and licking in pleas and sighs
Touching souls
Spiritually high
We grind
We grind.

the truth isn't always pretty
uplifting
or funny.
sometimes, it's painful
and haunting
but i tell you anyway.

the truth may not soothe your wounds.
it could bruise
or cut where you're healing too.
but i tell you anyway.

the truth may not be what you assumed
could be better
or worse than you expected.
it may make you sympathetic
or completely apathetic.
but I tell you anyway.

the truth may not make me more loveable
or beautiful or desirable.
but i tell you anyway.

the truth is
i'm always evolving and choosing.
pain is
one of my muses.
the truth is
i've made choices i regret
i struggle to live without guilt
i struggle to be all of myself
i struggle to embrace what i've built
i struggle not to be destructive.

i hope the truth won't end our relationship
though sometimes i fear it will
and yet
i expect you to stay
hope you will stay.
because no matter what the truth is
i tell you anyway.

What is the difference between
Acceptance and settling
Speaking affirmation
And ignoring the truth
Being positive
And being delusional
Being forgiving
And being a doormat
Not always needing to be right
And becoming the scapegoat
Supporting and enabling
Healing and fixing?
What is the hard and fast rule
To determine the difference
Between complacency
And unconditional love
Ignorance and bliss?
Baby?
What is this?

she understood widelegged bumble fuck talk
but spoke harvard british like her first language
couldn't be recognized in a crowd
couldn't be lost in one either
she understood things
said things
loved things.
hurt.
hurt things.

she spoke some mumbo jumbo shit
like some passionate romeo
from a shakespeare play
but she had more play
and even more tragedy.
she had dreams
and ghosts
and real drama.
she had sadness that gulfed the climaxes
she made you have.
she moaned and came releasing breaths
that made you cry
and feel safe enough to be yourself.
she made you feel new and free
like love could be.
made you feel like you had gotten inside
and she had gotten inside
you.
said things like
she would kill you if you left.
so where was she
a woman who thought she was her woman
might ask herself

on too many occasions when
her cell
went straight to voicemail.

i prefer heated conversations
where we do not jab each other's spirits
with name calling.
where we remain vulnerable
and speak our own truths
while attempting to understand each other
remembering we are lovers
as much as we desperately argue
to be understood.

i hate being afraid to speak
afraid to disturb the peace
when you haven't fully explained
and dismiss questioning
by being mentally and spiritually so far away
your touch is strange
and i can't find my way
back to you
to us.
even when your face
is buried beneath my waist
this word
i'm moaning
feels foreign.
but i'm
calling
your name
cumming
and gone.
can you hear me?

she speaks the way i write
sometimes, brutally honest without consideration
for the consequences of her words.

she speaks the way i write
sometimes rehearsed and calculated
sometimes hypothetical
always patient.
she tests theories by measuring behaviors.
every time she determines (y)
her lover becomes an (x).
so she's still seeking a solution to that equation.
frustrated
by all the women proud to be
50% of their math
searching outside of themselves
for another half
when we are all wholes
there are no fractions of soul
we are all
infinitely bright
but too many of us are
dimming our lights
by
not seeking inside,
first,
the courage to shine.

she speaks the way i write
in a stream of consciousness
spiritually connected
fearless
observant

and discerning
gravid
in the name of words
sounds
energy transferred
shared or igniting
have left her unwelcomed
by spirits fighting
to keep on
sleeping on their potential greatness.
while being invited
love requited
by those praying for an awakening
she is compelled
to be a phone ringing
to get out of the matrix.

she speaks the way i write
perceived edgy, dark and pessimistic
because she delivers truth
objectively explicit.
encouraging and encouraged
only at the throne of a revelation.
sowing tears as spiritual libation
she worships the truth
as divine
without fear of literature gods
and their master slave salvation.
she speaks the way i write.

She opens me
Makes me a portal
Connecting places
I cannot anchor
Or land.
Neither here
Nor there.

Early Riser

Last night
I was anchored.
A child in womb
No concept of a world beyond
Your arms.
Without want or desire
You ignite and extinguish my fire.
We are
Kindling
Fire
Against the cold.
Bound souls.
The scent of you disarming
Until the sun rises
Clocks alarming
I'm always learning
How to abandon paradise
And put back on my armor.
Good morning.

Warrior.

War.
She was
Destructive
Rebuilding
Hurting
Healing.
Afraid
Brave
Believing
Seeking
Dreaming
Being
Willing to fight for freedom
Still defining its meaning.
She'd hurt me
To free me.

"Cum for me, baby."
She conjures
Escaping
Between my thighs
In pleas and sighs
Bracing
To ride
My flesh
If I can't drive
Myself.
Penetrated
My spirit
Speaks her name
In other realms.

Warrior.
War.
She was
Always
Wearing armor.
Armed Sage
Charming
Willing to engage
Disarming me
In our exchange.
She sincerely came
For me.

Seductive.
Protecting me
From her own destruction.
Unless I requested, she fuck me.
Then she'd sculpt me
With the shards from her heart.
Make me her god
Then bare witness.
Worship is solvent.
Challenging life's hopelessness
With the light of death's openness
Blessing emptiness
With securer bridges
To evolve.
Pledging our loyalty
Committed to evolving
Pleasant is suffering
Pain is royalty's
Payment for wisdom.

Love as religion
Scripture says forgiveness
We cum together
On an altar of intuition
Prayed for
Meditated on
Faithfully
Saving
Saviors
Passion
Crucifixion.
We kill our egos
In spiritual submission.
To love, how our souls envisioned.

Love,
I never spoke to God about you
Never spoke to God while with you
Always trying to make sense
Of this spiritual connection in my flesh.
You had been hurt too much
To be approached or handled with anything less
Than divinity.

Nik Nicholson is an author, poet, education performer, content editor and painter. Her short stories and poems are featured in several anthologies. Her novel, Descendants of Hagar, won the 2013 Lambda Literary LGBT Debut Fiction Award. It's the first of a two-part series, which also includes Daughter of Zion, about a woman coming to terms with her masculinity during the early 1900's.

In 2015, Nicholson was awarded the Regional Artist Support Grant for 2015. Which funded research in Harlem for her second novel, Daughter of Zion. Daughter of Zion is scheduled to be released in the summer of 2017.

Web home: http://www.niknicholson.com
Facebook: http://www.facebook.com/ArtistNik
Twitter: http://www.twitter.com/artistnik
Instagram: http://www.instagram.com/artistnikn